THE FOOL'S JOURNEY

PART I: THE AWAKENING

RISHIK HAKIM

To Maa Tara, the Divine Mother of the Tarot, whose boundless wisdom and compassion guide us through the mysteries of life.

This book is dedicated to you, the embodiment of the eternal truth, which illuminates the path of seekers with your light. May your presence inspire, protect, and lead all who embark on their journeys of discovery and transformation.

In your name, may these pages serve as a bridge to the divine, helping others to connect with the sacred wisdom that flows from your eternal wellspring.

Contents

Preface

In every journey, there comes a moment when the seeker must pause, reflect, and take stock of the path traveled. This book is born out of such a moment in my life—a moment of deep introspection, spiritual inquiry, and the desire to share the wisdom that has guided me along the way.

I have always been drawn to the mysteries of the universe, the hidden truths that lie beneath the surface of everyday life. My fascination with the esoteric, the mystical, and the spiritual has led me down many paths, but none as profound as my connection with the ancient wisdom of the Tarot. Over time, I have come to understand that the Tarot is not just a tool for divination, but a reflection of the soul's journey, a map that guides us through the cycles of life, death, and rebirth.

This book is dedicated to Maa Tara, the divine mother of the Tarot and one of the goddesses of the Das Mahavidya. Her presence has been a guiding light in my life, offering wisdom, protection, and insight into the deeper layers of existence. It is through her grace that I have been able to explore the depths of the Tarot and bring forth the stories and lessons contained within these pages.

As you embark on this journey through the Tarot, I invite you to walk alongside the Fool, to experience the trials, tribulations, and triumphs that are part of every soul's path. Whether you are a seasoned reader of the Tarot or a curious newcomer, I hope that this book offers you not only guidance and inspiration but also a deeper connection to the divine forces that shape our lives.

Thank you for joining me on this journey. May the wisdom of the Tarot and the blessings of Maa Tara illuminate your path.

With gratitude and love,

Rishik Hakim (nom de plume)

Prologue

In the stillness before dawn, when the world is cloaked in shadows and the veil between realms is thin, a figure stands at the edge of the known world. This figure is the Fool, a traveler with no name and no destination, poised on the brink of an ancient cliff that overlooks the vast expanse of the unknown. The Fool carries nothing but a small, worn pack slung over one shoulder and a heart full of questions.

Above him, the sky is a canvas of deep indigo, dotted with stars that flicker like distant lanterns, guiding the way. The air is cool, tinged with the scent of earth and the promise of a new beginning. At the Fool's side, a sprightly dog barks excitedly, sensing the adventure that awaits.

But it is not the horizon that holds the Fool's gaze. Instead, his eyes are drawn to the figure that has appeared before him, emerging from the mist like a dream-made flesh. She is both familiar and otherworldly, her deep blue skin glowing softly in the twilight, her three eyes seeing far beyond the ordinary. This is Maa Tara, the divine mother of the Tarot, the guardian of the mysteries that the Fool is about to uncover.

She smiles gently, a gesture that is both comforting and enigmatic as if she knows the journey that lies ahead but will not reveal its secrets too soon. In her hands, she holds a small, shimmering compass, its needle spinning slowly before pointing toward the vast unknown.

With a voice that resonates with the power of the cosmos, Maa Tara speaks, "You stand at the threshold of a great journey, one that will take you through the realms of the seen and the unseen, the known and the unknown. But fear not, for I will be with you, guiding you as you walk the path of the Tarot. Trust in the compass I give you, for it will lead you where you need to go, even when the stars fade and the way is dark."

The Fool reaches out, taking the compass with a sense of awe and reverence. He feels a surge of resolve, a newfound courage to step into the unknown and embrace whatever the journey may bring.

As the first light of dawn begins to touch the sky, the Fool takes a deep breath, his heart full of anticipation. With one final look at Maa Tara, who nods in silent encouragement, the Fool steps forward, leaving the edge of the cliff and venturing into the vast expanse that lies ahead.

The journey of a thousand lifetimes begins with this first step, and the Fool knows that he is not alone. For with each step he takes, he carries the wisdom of the Tarot, the blessings of Maa Tara, and the promise of discovery, transformation, and enlightenment.

And so, the story begins...

CHAPTER ONE

The Beginning - The Fool (0)

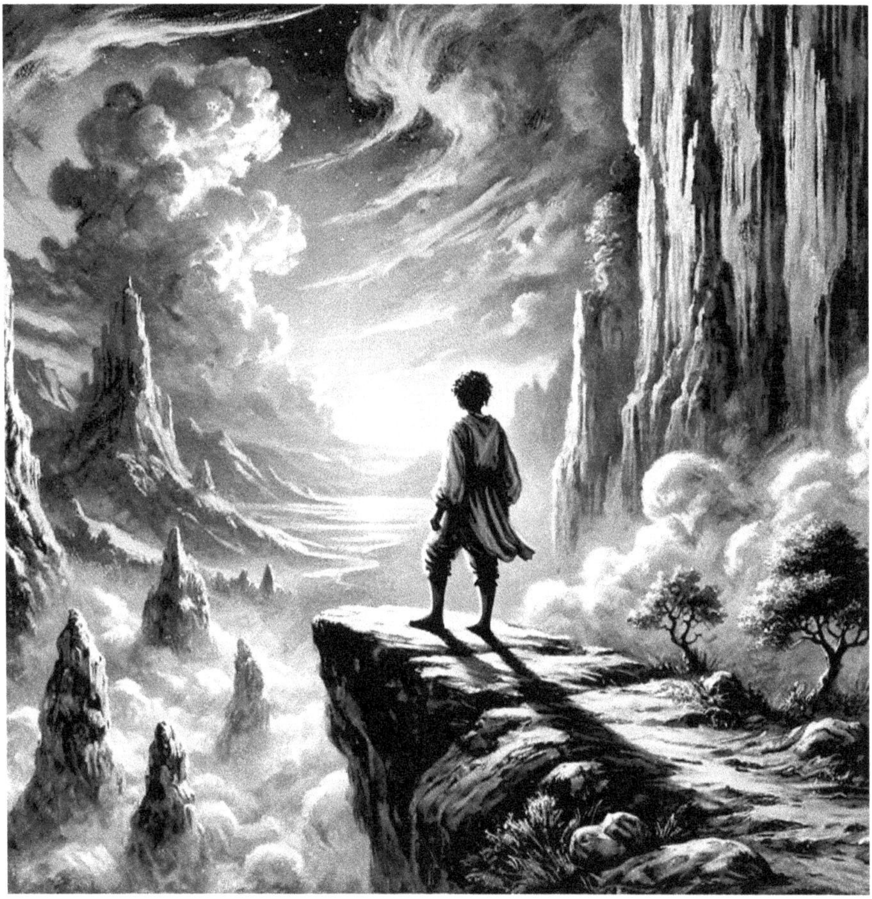

In the ever-shifting landscape where dreams blur into reality, our tale begins with a young wanderer known only as the Fool. On this morning, the sun painted the skies with strokes of orange and pink, casting a warm glow over the edge of the world. It was here, at the very brink of the known lands, that the Fool stood, his toes teasing the precipice of an ancient cliff.

The Call to Adventure

With nothing but a small, worn pack filled with essentials and trinkets, the Fool hummed an old, forgotten tune, the kind that stirred the heart to yearn for distant places. At his side, a sprightly little dog, his loyal companion, danced around in circles, barking with excitement.

"Ah, my little friend," the Fool chuckled, bending down to scratch the dog's ears. "It seems the horizon calls us both. What say you, shall we discover what lies beyond?"

The dog yapped in approval, its tail wagging like a tiny flag caught in a breeze.

A Leap of Faith

Taking a deep breath, the Fool looked out across the vast unknown. The wind whispered secrets in his ear, tales of hidden wonders and worlds awaiting his footprints.

"Just think of the stories we'll tell, the mysteries we'll unravel!" the Fool exclaimed aloud, more to the wind than to his canine friend. His heart swelled with a cocktail of excitement and nervousness.

As he stood there, lost in thought, an old woman approached him. Her hair was as white as the snow-capped mountains in the distance, and her eyes held the calm of the deep sea.

"Young traveler," she said, her voice gentle yet carrying an edge of warning, "the path you choose is fraught with shadows and light, joy and despair. Are you prepared for the journey that awaits?"

The Fool turned to her, his smile unwavering. "Oh, wise mother, I am but an empty vessel eager to be filled. What is life, if not a grand adventure, a chance to taste the sweet and bitter on one's tongue?"

The old woman nodded, her gaze softening. "Indeed, it is as you say. Remember, every step is a lesson. Go forth with an open heart and courage. The road will teach you what you need to know."

With those enigmatic words, she handed him a small, shimmering compass. "This will guide you when the stars fade. Trust it as you trust the beating of your heart."

Grasping the compass, the Fool felt a surge of resolve. "Thank you, kind mother. I shall cherish this gift and the wisdom it brings."

Into the Unknown

With the compass in his pocket and his dog eagerly bounding ahead, the Fool finally took his first step forward. The ground beneath him seemed to welcome his weight, firm and promising.

"Come, my friend!" he called to his dog, his voice ringing with thrill. "Let us find the stories waiting in the silence of the unexplored!"

The path curled into the morning mist like a secret waiting to be whispered. And as the Fool disappeared into the veil of fog, his laughter echoed back, mingling with the old woman's murmured blessings.

Thus, with the world sprawling before him like a canvas yet to be painted, the Fool ventured forth, driven by the raw beauty of the unknown and the pure joy of discovery. Each step was a story, each breath a chapter, and the road—endless.

CHAPTER TWO

THE MAGICIAN - MASTERY OF ELEMENTS

As the Fool ventured deeper into the realms of the unknown, the path wound through a lush, verdant forest. The sunlight trickled through the leaves, casting a mosaic of shadows and light upon the ground. It was in this dappled glade that the Fool's journey took a significant turn. For there, amidst the ancient trees, he encountered a figure as enigmatic as the forest itself—the Magician.

The Meeting

The Magician stood by a stone table cluttered with curious objects: a wand, a pentacle, a cup, and a sword—each representing the elements of air, earth, water, and fire. His eyes, sharp and piercing, seemed to hold the mysteries of the ages.

"Ah, a traveler emerges from the mists of possibility," the Magician greeted, his voice both welcoming and cryptic. "What brings you to the crossroads of fate and free will?"

The Fool, intrigued and slightly bewildered, approached the table. "I seek to understand the depths of life, the secrets that elude the grasp of common men."

The Lesson

The Magician smiled, a knowing twist to his lips. "You seek wisdom, yet it is not something that is given, but rather something that is earned. Watch closely."

With a graceful motion, the Magician waved his hand over the table. The objects began to levitate, circling gracefully above the wood. "Each of these," he explained, "represents the essential elements of the universe. To master them is to understand the very fabric of existence."

The Fool watched, mesmerized by the dance of the elements. "How does one begin to master such forces?" he asked, his voice tinged with awe.

"By understanding that all external mastery begins with internal control," the Magician replied. He pointed to his head and then to his heart. "Mind and spirit. Knowledge and passion. Control these, and you command the world."

The Advice

The Magician lowered the elements back onto the table and fixed his gaze on the Fool. "You have embarked on a noble journey, young seeker. But beware, the path is strewn with both creation and destruction. Each step forward is a choice. Each choice, a destiny forged."

The Fool absorbed these words, feeling the weight of their meaning. "And how will I know if I'm making the right choices?" he asked.

"With this," the Magician said, handing the Fool a small, ornate mirror. "Look into this when doubt shadows your heart. It will show you not what you wish to see, but what you need to see."

The Departure

Grateful for the profound encounter, the Fool tucked the mirror into his pack. "Thank you, wise Magician. May our paths cross again in the tapestry of time."

"As they will," the Magician assured with a cryptic smile. "For every end is but a new beginning in the spiral of life."

With a respectful nod, the Fool continued on his path, each step echoing with the newfound knowledge of the elements and the internal mastery they required. Behind him, the Magician watched, a silent guardian of the crossroads, his eyes twinkling with the secret joy of a teacher whose lessons had found fertile ground.

CHAPTER THREE

THE HIGH PRIESTESS - THE GATEWAY TO THE SUBCONSCIOUS

After parting ways with the Magician, the Fool continued his wanderings, his mind brimming with thoughts of elements and inner mastery. As he traversed a dense, moonlit forest, a sense of deep tranquility fell upon him, a stark contrast to the vibrant energy of his last encounter. It was here, under the silver glow of the moon, that the Fool came upon a serene lake, its surface as smooth as glass. Seated at its edge was a figure cloaked in midnight blue, her presence both calming and inscrutable—the High Priestess.

The Enigmatic Encounter

The High Priestess did not look up as the Fool approached, her eyes fixed on a thick, ancient tome resting on her lap. The air around her was thick with the scent of jasmine and myrrh, and a thin mist hovered over the lake's surface, adding to the surreal beauty of the scene. "Good evening, wise lady," the Fool greeted, his voice a whisper, lest he disturb the tranquil scene. Without lifting her gaze, the High Priestess spoke, her voice a melody that seemed to echo the mystic rhythms of the universe. "The evening is wise, but I am merely its student. What seeks you by the light of the moon?"

The Lesson of Intuition

The High Priestess closed her book softly and finally looked up, her eyes piercing the shadows between them. "Understanding is a pearl of great price, found deep within the oceans of our souls. To reach it, you must dive beneath the surface, into waters dark and daunting."

She gestured to the lake. "This water is like the mind, its surface but a reflection of the world. True knowledge lies beneath, in the quiet depths."

The Fool, intrigued, knelt beside her. "How does one dive into these depths?"

"With the key of intuition," she replied, pulling a small, silver key from the folds of her robe and handing it to him. "This key will unlock doors within you that lead to realms untold. But beware, for not all that dwells within is gentle and kind."

The Advice

The High Priestess stood, her form casting long shadows on the water. "The path you walk is layered, each step a descent deeper into your own essence. Trust your inner voice, even when it whispers, for it speaks the truth of your soul."

Taking the key, the Fool felt a shiver run through him—a mix of fear and anticipation. "And if I become lost?"

"Look to the moon," she said, pointing to the celestial orb above them. "Its light will guide you back to the paths you are meant to walk. Remember, every shadow is cast by a light."

The Departure

With a bow of gratitude, the Fool tucked the silver key into his pocket, its cool metal a comforting weight against his thigh. "Thank you for your wisdom, High Priestess. May your studies bring you closer to the mysteries you seek."

"As may your journey reveal the mysteries within you," she replied, her voice fading as she turned back to her tome and the lake, once more becoming a part of the ethereal landscape.

Filled with new reverence for the depths of his own mind, the Fool set off once again, the key not only a tool but a symbol of the courage needed to explore the unknown territories of his own being.

CHAPTER FOUR

THE EMPRESS - THE NURTURER OF LIFE

As the Fool journeyed further, the dense forest began to thin, giving way to a lush and fertile valley. The landscape changed gradually from the shadowy woods to a vibrant, sunlit expanse filled with blooming flowers, flowing rivers, and the sweet scent of ripe fruit. It was a land of abundance, where life flourished in every corner, and the air was filled with the songs of birds and the hum of bees.

In the heart of this paradise, the Fool encountered a figure unlike any he had met before. Seated on a throne adorned with vines and blossoms, was the Empress. She radiated a warmth that seemed to nurture the very earth beneath her feet. Her gown was woven from the softest silks, embroidered with patterns of wheat and roses, and a crown of twelve stars rested upon her head, symbolizing her connection to the celestial and the earthly realms.

The Meeting

The Empress looked up as the Fool approached, her eyes filled with a gentle kindness that immediately put him at ease. She held a scepter in one hand, representing her dominion over nature and life, while her other hand rested lightly on her swelling belly, suggesting the promise of new life.

"Welcome, traveler," she said, her voice as soothing as a summer breeze. "You have come far and learned much, but there is more you must understand before you can continue on your journey."

The Fool, feeling the warmth of her presence, bowed respectfully. "I seek to understand the forces that give life its richness and beauty. What can you teach me, gracious lady?"

The Lesson of Abundance

The Empress smiled and gestured to the flourishing landscape around them. "All that you see here is the result of love, care, and patience. I am the embodiment of creation, the force that nurtures life and brings it into being. But remember, true abundance is not merely material wealth; it is the richness of the spirit, the ability to give and receive love, to create and nurture life in all its forms."

She stood and moved towards a nearby tree, laden with ripe fruit. With a simple gesture, she plucked a fruit and offered it to the Fool. "Take this," she said. "It is a symbol of the nourishment that life offers, the sustenance not just for the body but for the soul. In your journey, you will encounter many who are hungry—not just for food, but for love, kindness, and understanding. It is your task to nourish them as you nourish yourself."

The Fool accepted the fruit, feeling its weight and the life it contained. He realized that the Empress was teaching him about the importance of balance, of giving and receiving, of understanding the cycles of life and growth.

The Advice

The Empress placed a hand on the Fool's shoulder, her touch warm and comforting. "Remember, dear traveler, that to create is to embody the divine. Whether you are sowing seeds in the earth or in the hearts of others, you are participating in the eternal dance of life. Be a gardener of the soul, tending to the seeds of love, creativity, and compassion wherever you go."

She looked up at the sky, where the sun was beginning to set, casting a golden glow over the valley. "Your journey will take you to places both beautiful and barren, but always carry within you the understanding that you have the power to create and nurture life. This is the gift I bestow upon you—the knowledge that you are a creator, capable of bringing beauty and love into the world."

The Fool, deeply moved by her words, bowed once more. "Thank you, Empress. I will carry your wisdom with me and strive to be worthy of the gift you have given."

The Departure

As the Fool turned to leave, the Empress returned to her throne, her presence as nurturing and serene as the valley she ruled. The path before him now seemed clearer, illuminated by the understanding of the power he held within himself to create and nurture, to bring light and life wherever he went.

With a renewed sense of purpose, the Fool continued his journey, the lessons of the Empress echoing in his heart. He now understood that his path was not just about seeking knowledge and mastering the elements, but also about nurturing the world around him, just as the Empress nurtured the valley.

CHAPTER FIVE

THE EMPEROR - THE ARCHITECT OF ORDER

Leaving the fertile valley of the Empress behind, the Fool journeyed onward, feeling the warmth of her wisdom still resonating within him. The landscape gradually changed from a lush, nurturing environment to one that was more structured and disciplined. The path ahead led into a vast, well-organized kingdom where every stone seemed to be placed with intention, and every road led with purpose.

At the center of this kingdom, the Fool encountered a grand fortress, built of strong stone and towering above the surrounding lands. Inside, seated upon a throne carved from the same unyielding rock, was a figure who exuded authority and strength—the Emperor.

The Meeting

The Emperor was a commanding presence, dressed in robes of rich red and adorned with symbols of power and stability. His gaze was steady, his posture unyielding. In his right hand, he held a scepter, symbolizing his dominion, while in his left rested an orb, representing the world he governed.

"Welcome, traveler," the Emperor said, his voice firm yet not unkind. "You have come far, and now you stand before the seat of order and authority. What is it that you seek?"

The Fool, feeling the weight of the Emperor's gaze, replied, "I seek to understand the structure that governs life, the laws that give form to the world and maintain balance."

The Lesson of Authority and Structure

The Emperor nodded approvingly. "Order and structure are the foundations upon which all things are built. Without them, there is only chaos. As the Empress nurtures and gives life, I provide the framework within which that life can thrive. My role is to protect, to establish boundaries, and to ensure that the laws of the land are upheld."

He gestured to the vast kingdom beyond the fortress walls. "Look upon my realm. It is orderly, disciplined, and secure. Every decision I make is with the intent to preserve harmony and stability. But know this: authority is not just about power; it is about responsibility. To lead is to serve, to ensure the welfare of all within your domain."

The Fool listened intently, understanding that the Emperor's teachings were about more than just ruling a land—they were about mastering the self, creating order within, and setting boundaries that would allow him to grow and thrive.

The Advice

The Emperor leaned forward, his expression becoming more personal, almost fatherly. "You must learn to govern yourself with the same care and discipline with which I govern this kingdom. Set clear goals, establish your principles, and be steadfast in your decisions. But do not confuse rigidity with strength. True power lies in knowing when to bend without breaking."

He handed the Fool a small, intricately carved stone, smooth and polished. "This stone represents the foundation you must build within yourself. It is solid, enduring, yet it can also be shaped by the forces you apply to it. Let it remind you that you are the architect of your own life, responsible for the structures you create within and around you."

The Fool accepted the stone, feeling its cool weight in his hand. He understood now that just as the Empress had taught him to nurture and create, the Emperor was teaching him the importance of building a strong foundation, of creating order out of chaos.

The Departure

As the Fool prepared to leave, the Emperor stood, placing a firm yet encouraging hand on his shoulder. "Go forth, traveler, and remember that with great power comes great responsibility. You are not just a wanderer; you are a builder, a protector of the order you create. Let your actions be guided by wisdom and justice, and you will find that even the wildest of dreams can be brought into reality through structure and discipline."

With these words echoing in his mind, the Fool departed from the fortress, the stone in his hand a constant reminder of the Emperor's lessons. As he walked away, he felt a new sense of strength and purpose, knowing that his journey was not just about exploration, but also about building a life of meaning, grounded in the principles of order and responsibility.

The path ahead, once chaotic and uncertain, now appeared more defined, as if shaped by the very hand of the Emperor himself. And so, the Fool continued on his journey, ready to embrace the challenges that lay ahead with the wisdom of the Empress and the strength of the Emperor guiding his every step.

CHAPTER SIX

THE HIEROPHANT - THE KEEPER OF WISDOM

With the Emperor's lessons of structure and authority still fresh in his mind, the Fool continued his journey, feeling more grounded and aware of the importance of discipline and order. As he traveled further, the landscape began to change once again. The roads led him to a place where the air was thick with the scent of incense, and the sounds of chanting echoed through the valleys. The architecture here was grand and ancient, with towering spires that seemed to touch the heavens, adorned with sacred symbols and intricate carvings.

At the center of this sacred place stood a grand temple, its doors open wide as if inviting those who sought knowledge and spiritual guidance. The Fool, drawn by an unseen force, entered the temple with a sense of reverence and curiosity. Inside, the light was dim, filtered through stained glass windows that cast colorful patterns on the stone floor. The atmosphere was hushed, filled with the weight of centuries of devotion and study.

Seated upon an ornate throne, dressed in ceremonial robes and holding a staff of authority, was the Hierophant—a figure who exuded an aura of deep wisdom and spiritual insight. His presence was both comforting and commanding, a bridge between the divine and the earthly.

The Meeting

The Hierophant looked up as the Fool approached, his eyes filled with the knowledge of countless lifetimes. "Welcome, seeker," he said, his voice resonating with a calm authority. "You have journeyed far and learned much, but now you stand before the gateway of higher wisdom. What is it that you seek?"

The Fool, feeling the sacredness of the space, bowed respectfully. "I seek to understand the spiritual laws that govern our existence, the wisdom that has been passed down through the ages. How can I align myself with the greater truths of the universe?"

The Lesson of Spiritual Guidance

The Hierophant smiled gently, his expression one of patient understanding. "To seek wisdom is a noble pursuit, but true wisdom is not just knowledge—it is understanding, it is faith, and it is the ability to see the divine in all things. I am the keeper of sacred traditions, the guide who helps others find their path to enlightenment."

He gestured to the symbols around the temple, each one representing different aspects of the divine. "These symbols, these rituals, they are the keys that unlock the mysteries of the universe. But they are only the beginning. True wisdom comes from within, from a deep connection to the divine that transcends words and teachings."

The Fool listened closely, realizing that the Hierophant was teaching him about the importance of spiritual discipline, of understanding the deeper meaning behind the rituals and traditions that had been passed down through generations.

The Advice

The Hierophant stood, his movements graceful and deliberate, and approached the Fool. "To align yourself with the greater truths, you must be open to learning, to questioning, and to growing. But remember, wisdom is not just for yourself; it is to be shared, to guide others on their path. As you continue your journey, seek out teachers, but also be a teacher to those who are lost."

He placed a hand on the Fool's head in a gesture of blessing. "Trust in the divine order, in the teachings that have stood the test of time, but also in your own inner wisdom. The key to enlightenment is not just in the scriptures or the rituals, but in the way you live your life, in the love and compassion you show to others."

The Fool felt a profound sense of peace and clarity as the Hierophant spoke. He understood now that his journey was not just about personal growth, but also about understanding his place in the greater tapestry of existence, and the responsibility he had to pass on the wisdom he acquired.

The Departure

As the Fool prepared to leave, the Hierophant returned to his throne, his presence as serene and wise as when the Fool had first entered. "Go forth, seeker, and remember that the path to wisdom is never-ending. It is a journey that requires patience, humility, and a deep reverence for the mysteries of the universe. May your steps be guided by the light of truth and the love of the divine."

The Fool bowed deeply, feeling a deep respect and gratitude for the Hierophant's teachings. As he left the temple, the sacred symbols and the scent of incense lingering in his mind, he felt a renewed sense of purpose. He was not just a traveler on a journey of self-discovery; he was a seeker of wisdom, a student of the divine, and a guide for others who sought the light.

The road ahead was long and winding, but the Fool walked with a newfound sense of direction, knowing that he carried with him the blessings of the Hierophant and the sacred teachings of those who had come before him. He was ready to continue his journey, armed with the knowledge that true wisdom was a gift to be shared, a light to be passed from one soul to another, illuminating the path for all who seek the truth.

CHAPTER SEVEN

THE LOVERS - THE POWER OF CHOICE

With the Hierophant's blessings and teachings still resonating within him, the Fool continued his journey, feeling more connected to the spiritual world and the wisdom of the ages. The road ahead began to change once more, leading him through a landscape that was both lush and inviting. The air was warm, filled with the scent of blooming flowers, and the sound of a gentle breeze rustling through the trees.

As the Fool walked, he came to a fork in the path. One road led up a hill towards a towering mountain, its peak lost in the clouds, while the other wound down into a verdant valley where a river glistened in the sunlight. It was here, at this crossroads, that the Fool encountered a scene unlike any he had seen before.

In the center of the crossroads stood two figures—a man and a woman. They were both radiant, their expressions serene and filled with an unmistakable bond that seemed to transcend mere physical connection. Behind the man stood a tree laden with fruit, and behind the woman, a tree with a serpent coiled around its trunk. Above them hovered a majestic angel, wings spread wide, casting a protective light over the scene.

The Meeting

As the Fool approached, the angel looked down upon him with eyes full of compassion and understanding. "Welcome, traveler," the angel said, their voice soft yet resonant. "You stand at a crossroads, a place where choices must be made, and paths must be chosen. What is it that you seek?"

The Fool, feeling the weight of the moment, replied, "I seek to understand the nature of love and the choices that shape our lives. How do we know which path to take, which decisions will lead us to fulfillment?"

The Lesson of Choice and Love

The angel smiled gently, gesturing towards the two figures. "These are the Lovers, a symbol of the power of choice and the union of opposites. Their love is not just physical, but a deep spiritual connection that binds them together. Yet, with love comes the necessity of choice, and with choice comes the responsibility of understanding the consequences of our decisions."

The angel's gaze turned towards the man and the woman. "The man represents the conscious mind, seeking truth and knowledge, while the woman symbolizes the subconscious, intuition, and the mysteries of the heart. The trees behind them are symbols of the choices we face—the tree of knowledge and the tree of life. The serpent, a symbol of temptation, reminds us that not all choices are simple or without consequence."

The Fool listened closely, realizing that the lesson here was not just about love, but about the choices that define our lives. The angel was teaching him that every decision we make is a step on our path, shaping who we are and who we will become.

The Advice

The angel stepped closer to the Fool, their presence comforting and wise. "In your journey, you will face many choices, and not all will be easy. But remember this: true love, true fulfillment, comes from making choices that are in harmony with your highest self, that align with your deepest values and desires."

The angel placed a gentle hand on the Fool's shoulder. "When you are faced with a difficult decision, look within yourself. Trust your intuition, but also use your mind to weigh the consequences. Seek a balance between heart and mind, passion and reason. And above all, remember that love, in all its forms, is the greatest force in the universe. It has the power to heal, to unite, and to guide you on your path."

The Fool felt a deep sense of peace and clarity as the angel spoke. He understood now that the choices he made were not just about the path he walked, but about the person he was becoming. The Lovers were a reminder that love and choice were intertwined, each shaping the other in the dance of life.

The Departure

As the Fool prepared to leave, the angel returned to their place above the Lovers, their wings casting a protective light over the scene. "Go forth, traveler, and remember that every choice you make is a reflection of your soul. Choose wisely, with love and with purpose, and you will find that your path will lead you to the fulfillment you seek."

The Fool bowed deeply, feeling a profound gratitude for the angel's wisdom. As he walked away from the crossroads, he glanced back at the Lovers, their hands intertwined, their bond unbreakable. He knew now that his journey was not just about the external world, but about the choices he made within, the love he carried in his heart, and the path he chose to walk.

With a renewed sense of purpose, the Fool continued on his journey, the lessons of the Lovers guiding his every step. He understood that life was a series of choices, each one leading him closer to his true self, and that love, in all its forms, was the key to unlocking the deepest truths of the universe.

CHAPTER EIGHT

THE CHARIOT - THE TRIUMPH OF WILL

With the lessons of love and choice guiding him, the Fool journeyed onward, feeling more confident and centered in his path. The road ahead began to change, becoming steeper and more challenging, winding through rugged hills and sharp cliffs. As the terrain grew more difficult, the Fool felt a growing determination within himself, a desire to overcome whatever obstacles lay in his way.

The path eventually led him to the foot of a great mountain. At the base of this mountain stood a magnificent chariot, gleaming in the sunlight. The chariot was drawn by two powerful sphinxes—one black, the other white—each representing opposing forces of the universe. Standing tall and proud within the chariot was a figure of unwavering resolve and strength—the Charioteer.

The Meeting

The Charioteer looked down at the Fool with eyes full of focus and determination. He was dressed in armor, adorned with symbols of victory and conquest. In one hand, he held the reins that controlled the sphinxes, and in the other, he carried a scepter, symbolizing his authority and mastery over the forces that pulled his chariot.

"Welcome, traveler," the Charioteer said, his voice strong and commanding. "You have come far, but now you stand at the threshold of a new challenge. What is it that you seek?"

The Fool, feeling the weight of the Charioteer's presence, replied, "I seek to understand the power of will and determination, the strength needed to overcome the obstacles that lie ahead."

The Lesson of Willpower and Control

The Charioteer nodded, his expression serious. "The path to victory is not an easy one. It requires focus, discipline, and an unyielding will to succeed. The chariot you see before you represents the vehicle of your will, the means by which you can overcome any challenge. But know this: the road to triumph is fraught with obstacles, both external and internal."

He gestured to the sphinxes, who stood calm yet powerful, ready to move at the slightest command. "These sphinxes represent the dual forces of the universe—light and dark, positive and negative, conscious and unconscious. To master the chariot, you must master these forces, bringing them into harmony under your control. It is not enough to simply possess willpower; you must also know how to direct it, how to channel your energy towards your goals." The Fool listened intently, realizing that the Charioteer was teaching him about the power of self-control, about the importance of aligning his inner and outer worlds to achieve his goals.

The Advice

The Charioteer stepped down from the chariot, his presence commanding yet encouraging. "To succeed in your journey, you must learn to control your emotions, your thoughts, and your actions. Focus your mind, and let nothing deter you from your path. But also remember that true victory is not about conquering others, but about conquering yourself."

He handed the Fool the reins of the chariot, the leather cool and firm in his hands. "Take these reins, and know that you hold the power to steer your life in any direction you choose. The path ahead is yours to command, but you must be vigilant, for the forces of doubt and fear will always seek to pull you off course. Stay focused, stay determined, and you will find that nothing is impossible."

The Fool felt a surge of energy and determination as he took the reins. He understood now that the Chariot was not just a vehicle of transportation, but a symbol of his own willpower, of his ability to overcome any obstacle with focus and resolve.

The Departure

As the Fool prepared to leave, the Charioteer returned to his place within the chariot, his hands steady on the reins. "Go forth, traveler, and remember that you are the master of your own destiny. The road may be difficult, but with the power of your will, you can overcome any challenge that lies ahead. Let your determination guide you, and you will find that the triumphs you seek are within your grasp."

The Fool bowed deeply, feeling a deep respect for the Charioteer's teachings. As he climbed into the chariot, he felt a newfound strength and resolve, knowing that he had the power to steer his life in the direction of his choosing.

With the reins in hand, the Fool commanded the sphinxes to move forward. The chariot surged ahead, smooth and unstoppable, as if guided by an invisible force. The path ahead was steep and treacherous, but the Fool felt no fear, only a deep sense of purpose and determination.

As he rode onward, the lessons of the Charioteer echoed in his mind, reminding him that true victory came not from external conquests, but from mastering the forces within himself. The journey ahead was long, but the Fool knew that with the power of his will, there was nothing he could not overcome. And so, with the chariot as his guide, he continued on his path, ready to face whatever challenges lay ahead, knowing that the triumphs of the spirit were within his reach.

CHAPTER NINE

Strength - The Power of Inner Fortitude

The Fool, now emboldened by the Charioteer's lessons of willpower and determination, continued his journey. The path ahead grew less steep, leading him into a vast, open landscape. The air was calm, and the sun shone brightly, casting a warm, golden light over the fields. As he walked, the Fool felt a growing sense of peace and balance within himself, a quiet strength that seemed to come from deep within.

It was in this tranquil setting that the Fool encountered his next guide. In the middle of a field of wildflowers, he saw a woman of serene beauty, dressed in flowing white garments. Beside her stood a great lion, powerful and majestic, yet calm and at ease in her presence. The woman's touch was gentle, her hand resting lightly on the lion's mane, and in her other hand, she held a garland of flowers.

The Meeting

As the Fool approached, the woman looked up, her eyes filled with kindness and understanding. "Welcome, traveler," she said, her voice soft yet strong. "You have come far, and now you stand before the embodiment of Strength. What is it that you seek?"

The Fool, drawn to the peaceful aura of the woman and the lion, replied, "I seek to understand the nature of true strength, the power that lies within us to face our fears and overcome the challenges of life."

The Lesson of Inner Strength

The woman smiled, her expression one of deep wisdom. "Strength is not just physical power or brute force. It is the inner fortitude that allows us to face adversity with grace and courage. True strength comes from within, from a place of calm and balance, where the mind and heart work together in harmony."

She gestured to the lion, who looked up at the Fool with gentle eyes. "This lion represents the wild and instinctual parts of ourselves, the passions and desires that can sometimes overwhelm us. But when we approach these forces with love, patience, and understanding, we can tame them, harnessing their power without being consumed by it."

The Fool listened closely, realizing that the woman was teaching him about the importance of self-control, of finding strength not through domination, but through compassion and understanding.

The Advice

The woman took the garland of flowers and placed it gently around the lion's neck, a symbol of the balance between strength and gentleness. "Remember, traveler, that true strength is found in the ability to remain calm and centered, even in the face of great challenges. It is the courage to face your fears, to accept your weaknesses, and to move forward with compassion and integrity."

She approached the Fool and placed her hand over his heart. "The power you seek is already within you. It is the strength of your spirit, the courage of your convictions, and the love that you carry in your heart. When you learn to harness this inner strength, you will find that there is no challenge too great, no obstacle too formidable."

The Fool felt a deep sense of peace and reassurance as the woman spoke. He understood now that true strength was not about overpowering others, but about mastering oneself, about finding balance and harmony within.

The Departure

As the Fool prepared to leave, the woman returned to her place beside the lion, her presence as serene and powerful as ever. "Go forth, traveler, and remember that true strength is gentle, yet unyielding. It is the power to face the storms of life with a calm heart and a steady hand. Let your inner strength guide you, and you will find that you are capable of far more than you ever imagined."

The Fool bowed deeply, feeling a profound gratitude for the woman's teachings. As he walked away from the field, the image of the woman and the lion lingered in his mind, a reminder of the balance between strength and gentleness, between power and compassion.

With a renewed sense of purpose, the Fool continued on his journey, the lessons of Strength guiding his every step. He understood now that the challenges ahead would not be met with brute force, but with the quiet strength of his spirit, the courage to face his fears, and the wisdom to act with love and integrity.

The road ahead was long and uncertain, but the Fool walked with confidence, knowing that the true power he sought was not in the world around him, but within his own heart. And so, with the strength of his spirit as his guide, he continued on his path, ready to face whatever challenges lay ahead, knowing that with inner fortitude, there was nothing he could not overcome.

CHAPTER TEN

The Hermit - The Light of Inner Wisdom

With the lessons of inner strength guiding him, the Fool journeyed onward, feeling a deep sense of calm and resilience. As he ventured further, the landscape began to change once more, becoming more solitary and remote. The bustling sounds of life faded into the distance, replaced by the soft rustle of leaves and the whisper of the wind. The path grew narrower, leading the Fool into a mountainous region where the air was thin and cool.

It was in this quiet, isolated place that the Fool encountered the next figure on his journey. At the top of a steep, rocky hill stood a solitary figure cloaked in a long, gray robe. In one hand, the figure held a lantern, its light glowing faintly in the gathering dusk, while in the other hand, he carried a staff to aid his ascent.

This was the Hermit, a figure of profound introspection and solitude, whose eyes were deep pools of wisdom earned through years of quiet contemplation.

The Meeting

As the Fool approached, the Hermit looked up, his gaze penetrating yet gentle. His face was lined with age, but his expression was one of peace and understanding. "Welcome, traveler," the Hermit said, his voice soft and resonant, like the echo of distant mountains. "You have journeyed far, but now you stand at the threshold of deeper understanding. What is it that you seek?"

The Fool, feeling the weight of the solitude around him, replied, "I seek to understand the wisdom that comes from within, the knowledge that is found in solitude and reflection. How can I find the light of truth in the darkness of the unknown?"

The Lesson of Inner Wisdom

The Hermit nodded slowly, his lantern casting a soft glow over the rocky terrain. "The path to true wisdom is a solitary one, for it is in the quiet moments of reflection that we find the answers we seek. This lantern I carry represents the light of inner wisdom, the guiding flame that illuminates the darkness of ignorance and fear."

He gestured to the vast expanse of mountains and valleys below. "The world is full of noise and distractions, but true understanding comes from turning inward, from seeking the truth within yourself. In solitude, we confront our deepest fears, our greatest doubts, and in doing so, we find the strength to transcend them."

The Fool listened closely, realizing that the Hermit was teaching him about the importance of introspection, of taking the time to look within and find the answers that could not be found in the external world.

The Advice

The Hermit stepped closer, holding the lantern high so that its light illuminated the Fool's face. "Remember, traveler, that the journey to wisdom is not one that can be rushed. It requires patience, humility, and a willingness to be alone with your thoughts. But know this: the light of truth is always within you, even in the darkest moments."

He handed the lantern to the Fool, the metal cool against his skin. "Take this light with you as you continue your journey. Let it guide you through the shadows of doubt and fear, and remember that the answers you seek are not out there in the world, but within your own heart and mind."

The Fool felt a deep sense of gratitude and reverence as he took the lantern. He understood now that the path to true wisdom required solitude, introspection, and a willingness to face the darkness within.

The Departure

As the Fool prepared to leave, the Hermit returned to his solitary vigil, his presence as quiet and steadfast as the mountains around him. "Go forth, traveler, and remember that the light of wisdom is yours to carry. Let it guide you through the unknown, and trust in the truth that it reveals. The journey ahead is long, but with the light of inner wisdom, you will find your way."

The Fool bowed deeply, feeling a profound respect for the Hermit's teachings. As he walked away from the mountain, the lantern in his hand casting a warm, reassuring glow, he felt a renewed sense of purpose and clarity. He understood now that the journey was not just about exploring the world, but about exploring himself, about finding the answers that lay hidden within his own soul.

With the light of the Hermit's lantern guiding his steps, the Fool continued on his path, ready to face the darkness and the unknown with the wisdom and strength he had gained. He knew that the road ahead would not always be easy, but with the light of inner wisdom to guide him, there was nothing he could not overcome.

And so, with the lantern's glow illuminating the way, the Fool journeyed on, deeper into the mysteries of life, knowing that the answers he sought were within his grasp, waiting to be discovered in the quiet moments of reflection and solitude.

CHAPTER ELEVEN

THE WHEEL OF FORTUNE - THE CYCLES OF DESTINY

After his encounter with the Hermit, the Fool continued his journey, now more introspective and aware of the light within him that guided his path. The landscape around him began to change once again, transforming from the solitary heights of the mountains to a vast, open plain. The sky overhead was clear, but there was an unusual stillness in the air, as if the world was holding its breath, waiting for something to happen.

As the Fool walked, he noticed a large structure in the distance, unlike anything he had seen before. It was a massive wheel, standing upright in the middle of the plain, turning slowly and silently. The wheel was adorned with symbols and figures, each representing different aspects of life—fortune and misfortune, joy and sorrow, beginnings and endings.

Standing near the wheel was a figure cloaked in robes of deep blue, their face calm and enigmatic. This was the Keeper of the Wheel, the one who understood the cycles of life and the ever-turning nature of destiny.

The Meeting

As the Fool approached, the Keeper looked up, their eyes reflecting the wisdom of ages. "Welcome, traveler," the Keeper said, their voice echoing with the rhythm of the turning wheel. "You have journeyed far and faced many challenges, but now you stand before the Wheel of Fortune, the symbol of life's ever-changing cycles. What is it that you seek?"

The Fool, fascinated by the slow, deliberate movement of the wheel, replied, "I seek to understand the nature of destiny, the forces that govern our lives, and how we can navigate the changes that come our way."

The Lesson of Cycles and Change

The Keeper nodded, their gaze fixed on the wheel as it continued to turn. "Life is a series of cycles, each bringing its own challenges and opportunities. The Wheel of Fortune represents these cycles—the ups and downs, the moments of triumph and despair. No one can escape the turning of the wheel, for it is the nature of existence to change, to evolve."

They gestured to the symbols on the wheel, each one representing different stages of life. "There will be times when the wheel turns in your favor, when everything seems to go your way. But there will also be times when the wheel brings challenges, when you must face adversity and hardship. The key to navigating these cycles is to remain centered, to understand that nothing is permanent, and that all things are in a state of constant flux."

The Fool listened closely, realizing that the Keeper was teaching him about the impermanence of life, about the need to remain adaptable and resilient in the face of change.

The Advice

The Keeper stepped closer, their presence calm and reassuring. "When the wheel turns, it is easy to feel as though you are at the mercy of forces beyond your control. But remember, traveler, that you have the power to influence your own destiny. While you cannot stop the wheel from turning, you can choose how you respond to its movements. Embrace the cycles of life with grace, and you will find that even in the darkest moments, there is always the potential for growth and transformation."

They handed the Fool a small token, a replica of the wheel, made of silver and engraved with intricate symbols. "Take this with you as a reminder that life is ever-changing, and that with each turn of the wheel, new possibilities are born. Let it remind you to stay centered, to adapt to the changes that come your way, and to trust in the cycles of life."

The Fool accepted the token, feeling its weight and the significance it held. He understood now that the journey was not just about overcoming challenges, but about navigating the cycles of life with wisdom and grace.

The Departure

As the Fool prepared to leave, the Keeper returned to their place beside the wheel, their eyes still fixed on its slow, deliberate movement. "Go forth, traveler, and remember that life is a journey of cycles. Embrace the changes, learn from the challenges, and trust that the wheel will always turn in your favor if you remain true to yourself. The path ahead may be uncertain, but with each turn of the wheel, new opportunities await."

The Fool bowed deeply, feeling a deep respect for the Keeper's wisdom. As he walked away from the wheel, the token in his hand reflecting the light of the sun, he felt a renewed sense of purpose and clarity. He understood now that life was not a straight path, but a series of cycles, each bringing its own lessons and gifts.

With the Keeper's teachings in mind, the Fool continued on his journey, ready to face the cycles of life with resilience and grace. He knew that the road ahead would bring both joy and sorrow, triumph and defeat, but he also knew that with each turn of the wheel, he would grow stronger, wiser, and more in tune with the rhythms of the universe.

And so, with the Wheel of Fortune as his guide, the Fool journeyed on, embracing the cycles of destiny, ready to face whatever the future held, knowing that with each turn, he was moving closer to his true self and the fulfillment of his destiny.

CHAPTER TWELVE

JUSTICE – THE BALANCE OF TRUTH

With the Keeper of the Wheel's lessons on the cycles of life still resonating within him, the Fool continued his journey. The landscape gradually transformed, becoming more orderly and structured, with straight paths and symmetrical gardens lining the way. The air grew still, and a sense of solemnity filled the atmosphere. The Fool soon found himself approaching a grand temple, its façade adorned with symbols of scales and swords, representing balance, fairness, and the pursuit of truth.

At the entrance of the temple, seated on a marble throne, was a figure cloaked in robes of deep crimson, holding a pair of golden scales in one hand and an upright sword in the other. This was Justice, the embodiment of truth, fairness, and the moral order of the universe.

The Meeting

As the Fool approached, Justice looked down at him with piercing, unwavering eyes. Her expression was calm but serious, as if weighing the worth of all who came before her. "Welcome, traveler," Justice said, her voice steady and clear. "You have journeyed far and learned much, but now you stand before the seat of Justice, where truth is weighed and decisions are made. What is it that you seek?"

The Fool, feeling the weight of her gaze, replied, "I seek to understand the nature of justice and the role it plays in our lives. How can I live in alignment with truth and fairness in a world that often seems chaotic and unjust?"

The Lesson of Balance and Responsibility

Justice nodded, her eyes never leaving the Fool's. "Justice is the principle that ensures balance in the universe. It is the force that upholds fairness and truth, holding each individual accountable for their actions. The scales I hold represent this balance, the weighing of actions, intentions, and consequences. The sword represents the clarity and decisiveness needed to cut through illusion and reveal the truth."

She gestured to the scales, which tipped slightly as if measuring something unseen. "In your journey, you will face many situations where the line between right and wrong is blurred, where the truth is obscured by personal biases, emotions, and desires. To live justly, you must learn to weigh your decisions carefully, to consider not only your own needs but the needs of others, and to act with integrity and fairness in all that you do."

The Fool listened closely, realizing that Justice was teaching him about the importance of balance, of considering the consequences of his actions, and of living in alignment with universal truth.

The Advice

Justice leaned forward slightly, her gaze softening but remaining resolute. "Remember, traveler, that justice is not just about punishment or reward—it is about restoration, about bringing balance to situations that have fallen into disharmony. When you make decisions, ask yourself: Am I acting in a way that promotes fairness? Am I considering the impact of my actions on others? Am I being true to myself and to the principles I hold dear?"

She placed the scales gently in the Fool's hands, the golden metal cool and heavy. "Take these scales as a symbol of the balance you must strive to maintain in your life. Let them remind you that every action has a consequence, and that living justly requires constant vigilance and a commitment to the truth."

The Fool felt the weight of the scales and the responsibility they represented. He understood now that the journey was not just about seeking wisdom or achieving goals, but about living in a way that was fair, balanced, and true to the principles of justice.

The Departure

As the Fool prepared to leave, Justice returned to her upright position, the scales and sword once again held firmly in her hands. "Go forth, traveler, and remember that justice is the foundation of a harmonious life. Act with fairness, seek the truth in all things, and do not be swayed by anger, fear, or desire. The path ahead may challenge your sense of what is right, but with the scales of justice as your guide, you will find the strength to make the right choices."

The Fool bowed deeply, feeling a deep respect for Justice's teachings. As he walked away from the temple, the scales in his hands reflecting the light of the sun, he felt a renewed sense of purpose and clarity. He understood now that to live justly was to live in alignment with the truth, to act with integrity and fairness, and to uphold the balance in all things.

With Justice's teachings in mind, the Fool continued on his journey, ready to face the challenges of life with a clear sense of right and wrong. He knew that the road ahead would not always be easy, and that he would be faced with difficult decisions, but he also knew that with the scales of justice as his guide, he could navigate these challenges with wisdom and fairness.

And so, with the lessons of Justice firmly in his heart, the Fool journeyed on, seeking to live a life of balance, integrity, and truth, knowing that in doing so, he was contributing to the greater harmony of the universe.

CHAPTER THIRTEEN

THE HANGED MAN – THE POWER OF SURRENDER

With the scales of Justice guiding his actions, the Fool continued his journey, feeling more aligned with truth and fairness. The road ahead began to change once more, becoming narrow and winding as it led into a dense forest. The trees grew taller and closer together, their branches forming a canopy that blocked out much of the sunlight. The air was cool and still, and the only sounds were the rustling of leaves and the distant call of birds.

As the Fool ventured deeper into the forest, he noticed a strange sight up ahead. Hanging from a tree by one ankle was a man, suspended upside down. His hands were not bound, and his expression was one of calm and serenity, as if he had willingly placed himself in this position. The Fool approached cautiously, intrigued by the man's unusual posture and the aura of peace that surrounded him.

This was the Hanged Man, a figure who embodied the power of surrender, of seeing the world from a new perspective, and of finding wisdom in stillness and contemplation.

The Meeting

As the Fool approached, the Hanged Man opened his eyes and smiled gently, his expression serene and knowing. "Welcome, traveler," the Hanged Man said, his voice calm and soothing. "You have journeyed far and faced many challenges, but now you stand before the moment of surrender, the place where true insight is gained. What is it that you seek?"

The Fool, fascinated by the Hanged Man's unusual position, replied, "I seek to understand the power of surrender, of letting go and seeing the world from a different perspective. How can I find wisdom in stillness and learn to embrace the unknown?"

The Lesson of Surrender and Perspective

The Hanged Man nodded slowly, his body swaying gently in the breeze. "To surrender is not to give up, but to let go of the need for control, to trust in the flow of life and to see the world from a new angle. When we hang upside down, we see things that we could not see before, we gain insights that were hidden from our usual perspective."

He gestured to the forest around them, the trees towering above. "In the stillness of this moment, in the quiet surrender of our expectations and desires, we find clarity. We see the interconnectedness of all things, the patterns that guide our lives, and the deeper truths that lie beneath the surface."

The Fool listened closely, realizing that the Hanged Man was teaching him about the importance of letting go, of embracing uncertainty, and of finding wisdom in the places where we least expect it.

The Advice

The Hanged Man looked directly at the Fool, his eyes filled with gentle understanding. "Remember, traveler, that life is not always about action and control. There are times when we must surrender to the flow of life, when we must let go of our need to understand everything and allow ourselves to be guided by a higher wisdom."

He raised a hand, pointing to the sky above. "In those moments of surrender, when we let go of our resistance and our fear, we open ourselves to new possibilities, to new ways of seeing the world. Embrace the unknown, trust in the process, and know that sometimes the greatest insights come when we least expect them."

The Fool felt a deep sense of peace and acceptance as the Hanged Man spoke. He understood now that true wisdom often required letting go of his preconceived notions and allowing life to unfold in its own time.

The Departure

As the Fool prepared to leave, the Hanged Man remained suspended in his peaceful position, his presence as calm and serene as ever. "Go forth, traveler, and remember that the power of surrender is not a weakness, but a strength. It is the ability to let go, to trust in the flow of life, and to see the world from a new perspective. Let this lesson guide you on your journey, and you will find that even in the most uncertain moments, there is wisdom to be gained."

The Fool bowed deeply, feeling a profound respect for the Hanged Man's teachings. As he walked away from the tree, the image of the Hanged Man lingered in his mind, a reminder that sometimes the greatest strength lies in surrender, and that true insight often comes when we let go and allow ourselves to see the world from a different angle.

With the Hanged Man's lessons in mind, the Fool continued on his journey, ready to embrace the unknown and to find wisdom in the stillness and the surrender. He knew that the road ahead would bring challenges that required action and control, but he also knew that there would be times when he needed to step back, to let go, and to trust in the flow of life.

And so, with the power of surrender as his guide, the Fool journeyed on, ready to face whatever the future held, knowing that with each step, he was gaining a deeper understanding of himself and the world around him.

CHAPTER FOURTEEN

DEATH - THE TRANSFORMATION OF SELF

After his encounter with the Hanged Man, the Fool continued his journey, feeling a newfound sense of calm and acceptance. The path ahead was unclear, shrouded in a thick mist that seemed to rise from the earth itself. The air grew colder, and a sense of quiet inevitability settled over the landscape. The trees, once full of life, now stood bare, their leaves scattered on the ground like remnants of a forgotten season.

As the Fool walked through this eerie landscape, he noticed a figure emerging from the mist. This figure was draped in a long, black cloak, with a face obscured by shadows. In one hand, the figure held a scythe, and in the other, a single white rose. The presence of this figure was both unsettling and oddly comforting, as if it carried the weight of countless lifetimes and the promise of renewal.

This was Death, not as an end, but as a force of transformation and change—a figure who guided souls through the cycle of life, death, and rebirth.

The Meeting

As the Fool approached, Death turned to face him, revealing a skeletal face that was both haunting and serene. There was no malice in Death's gaze, only a deep, ancient understanding. "Welcome, traveler," Death said, their voice like the whisper of the wind through the trees. "You have journeyed far and faced many trials, but now you stand before the threshold of transformation. What is it that you seek?"

The Fool, feeling a mixture of fear and curiosity, replied, "I seek to understand the nature of death and transformation. How can I embrace change and let go of what no longer serves me?"

The Lesson of Transformation

Death nodded slowly, their movements deliberate and calm. "Death is not the end, but a necessary part of life. It is the force that clears away the old to make way for the new, the cycle that ensures the continuation of life and growth. To fear death is to fear change, but to embrace it is to understand the true nature of existence."

They held out the white rose, its delicate petals a stark contrast to the darkness around them. "This rose represents the purity and beauty of transformation, the promise that new life will always follow the end of the old. In your journey, you will face many endings—some will be painful, others will be liberating. But know that each ending is a beginning in disguise, a chance to shed the old and embrace the new."

The Fool listened closely, realizing that Death was teaching him about the importance of letting go, of allowing himself to be transformed by the experiences of life.

The Advice

Death stepped closer, their presence both comforting and commanding. "Remember, traveler, that transformation is not something to be feared, but something to be embraced. It is through change that we grow, that we evolve into the beings we are meant to become. When faced with loss or the end of something dear to you, do not cling to the past. Instead, open yourself to the possibilities of the future."

They handed the white rose to the Fool, the petals soft and cool against his skin. "Take this rose as a symbol of the beauty that lies in transformation. Let it remind you that every death, every ending, is but a step on the journey to new life. Embrace the changes that come your way, and trust that they are leading you to a higher purpose."

The Fool felt a deep sense of acceptance and peace as he took the rose. He understood now that death was not something to be feared, but a natural part of life's cycle, a force of renewal and transformation.

The Departure

As the Fool prepared to leave, Death returned to their place in the mist, their presence fading into the shadows. "Go forth, traveler, and remember that life is a journey of constant transformation. Embrace the changes that come, let go of what no longer serves you, and trust in the process of rebirth. The path ahead may be uncertain, but with each step, you are moving closer to your true self."

The Fool bowed deeply, feeling a profound respect for Death's teachings. As he walked away from the mist, the white rose in his hand a reminder of the lessons he had learned, he felt a renewed sense of purpose and clarity. He understood now that the journey was not just about seeking knowledge or achieving goals, but about embracing the transformations that life brought his way.

With Death's teachings in mind, the Fool continued on his journey, ready to face the challenges of life with an open heart and a willingness to change. He knew that the road ahead would bring both joy and sorrow, but he also knew that with each ending came the promise of a new beginning.

And so, with the white rose as his guide, the Fool journeyed on, embracing the transformations of life, ready to face whatever the future held, knowing that with each step, he was moving closer to the fulfillment of his destiny.

CHAPTER FIFTEEN

TEMPERANCE - THE ART OF BALANCE

With Death's teachings on transformation still fresh in his mind, the Fool continued his journey, feeling a renewed sense of purpose and clarity. The path ahead gradually shifted, leading him out of the shadowy forest and into a serene landscape bathed in soft, golden light. The air was warm and fragrant, filled with the scent of blooming flowers and the gentle sound of a babbling brook.

As he walked, the Fool noticed a figure standing by the edge of the water, calmly pouring liquid from one cup into another. The figure was androgynous, radiating an aura of peace and tranquility. They wore flowing robes of white and gold, and a pair of wings extended gracefully from their back. Behind them, a path led toward a distant mountain, where the sun was just beginning to rise.

This was Temperance, the embodiment of balance, harmony, and the blending of opposites.

The Meeting

As the Fool approached, Temperance looked up, their expression serene and welcoming. "Welcome, traveler," Temperance said, their voice as soothing as the gentle flow of water. "You have journeyed far and faced many transformations, but now you stand at the gateway of balance and harmony. What is it that you seek?"

The Fool, feeling the calming presence of Temperance, replied, "I seek to understand the art of balance, how to harmonize the different aspects of my life and find peace within myself. How can I learn to blend the opposing forces within me?"

The Lesson of Balance and Harmony

Temperance smiled gently, their hands continuing to pour the liquid from one cup to the other, the motion smooth and continuous. "Balance is the key to a harmonious life. It is the art of blending the opposing forces within and around us, of finding the middle path that brings peace and fulfillment. Just as I pour the water from one cup to another, you must learn to blend the different aspects of your life—your thoughts, emotions, desires, and actions—into a harmonious whole."

They gestured to the landscape around them, where the elements of earth, water, and sky seemed to blend seamlessly into one another. "In your journey, you will encounter many situations that challenge your sense of balance. There will be times when you feel pulled in different directions, when the forces within you seem to be at odds. But remember, true harmony comes from within, from your ability to integrate these forces and find the middle way."

The Fool listened closely, realizing that Temperance was teaching him about the importance of moderation, of finding the balance between extremes and living in harmony with himself and the world.

The Advice

Temperance stepped closer, their presence radiating calm and centeredness. "Remember, traveler, that balance is not something you achieve once and for all, but an ongoing practice, a dance of continuous adjustment. It requires patience, mindfulness, and the willingness to listen to the subtle cues of your body, mind, and spirit."

They handed the Fool one of the cups, the liquid within it clear and pure. "Take this as a reminder that life is a blending of many elements, each one contributing to the whole. Let it remind you to seek balance in all things—to moderate your actions, to harmonize your relationships, and to find the middle path that leads to peace and fulfillment."

The Fool felt a deep sense of calm and understanding as he took the cup. He understood now that true balance was not about rigid control, but about flexibility, adaptability, and the ability to flow with the currents of life.

The Departure

As the Fool prepared to leave, Temperance returned to their place by the water, their hands continuing the rhythmic motion of pouring. "Go forth, traveler, and remember that the art of balance is the key to a harmonious life. Seek the middle way, blend the forces within you, and find peace in the dance of opposites. The path ahead may bring challenges, but with the practice of balance, you will find your way through."

The Fool bowed deeply, feeling a profound respect for Temperance's teachings. As he walked away from the serene landscape, the cup in his hand a reminder of the lessons he had learned, he felt a renewed sense of peace and centeredness. He understood now that the journey was not just about achieving goals or overcoming challenges, but about finding harmony within himself and with the world around him.

With Temperance's teachings in mind, the Fool continued on his journey, ready to face the challenges of life with a balanced heart and a clear mind. He knew that the road ahead would bring both joy and sorrow, but he also knew that with the art of balance, he could navigate these challenges with grace and serenity.

And so, with the cup of harmony as his guide, the Fool journeyed on, seeking balance in all things, ready to face whatever the future held, knowing that with each step, he was moving closer to the fulfillment of his destiny.

CHAPTER SIXTEEN

THE DEVIL - THE CHAINS OF ILLUSION

With the teachings of Temperance guiding him, the Fool continued his journey, feeling more centered and balanced than ever before. The path ahead, however, began to change once more. The golden light of the serene landscape dimmed, giving way to shadows that seemed to stretch and twist in unnatural ways. The air grew thick and oppressive, filled with an uneasy tension that set the Fool on edge.

As he walked, the Fool found himself entering a dark, foreboding cave. The walls were lined with jagged rocks, and the air was heavy with the scent of smoke and sulfur. Deeper into the cave, the Fool could see a flickering, fiery glow, and as he approached, he saw a figure sitting on a massive stone throne, surrounded by chains and flames.

This was the Devil, a figure of temptation, bondage, and the dark forces that can ensnare the unwary. The Devil's presence was both intimidating and strangely alluring, a magnetic force that drew the Fool closer, even as a part of him wanted to turn and run.

The Meeting

As the Fool approached, the Devil looked up, a wicked smile playing on his lips. His eyes glowed with a fiery intensity, and his voice was smooth and seductive. "Welcome, traveler," the Devil said, his tone dripping with charm. "You have journeyed far and learned much, but now you stand at the crossroads of desire and freedom. What is it that you seek?"

The Fool, feeling a mixture of fear and curiosity, replied, "I seek to understand the nature of temptation, the chains that bind us to our lower selves, and how to break free from them. How can I avoid the traps of illusion and find true freedom?"

The Lesson of Illusion and Bondage

The Devil's smile widened, and he gestured to the chains that lay scattered around the cave. "These chains represent the illusions and temptations that bind us, the desires that keep us trapped in a cycle of addiction, fear, and ignorance. They are the forces that convince us that we are powerless, that we cannot break free from the patterns that hold us back."

He leaned forward, his eyes boring into the Fool's. "But the truth, traveler, is that these chains are of our own making. We create them through our thoughts, our fears, our desires. We give them power over us because we believe in the illusions they represent. The key to breaking free is to see these illusions for what they are—to recognize that the power lies within you, not in the chains that bind you."

The Fool listened closely, realizing that the Devil was teaching him about the dangers of attachment, of becoming enslaved to the desires and fears that cloud the mind and prevent true freedom.

The Advice

The Devil stood, his presence towering and imposing, but his voice was soft, almost whispering. "Remember, traveler, that the chains that bind you are not real—they are illusions, born of your own mind. To break free, you must confront your fears, your desires, and see them for what they truly are. Do not be deceived by appearances or temptations. Look deeper, and you will find that the power to free yourself has always been within you."

He handed the Fool a small, silver key, its surface cold and smooth to the touch. "Take this key as a symbol of your ability to unlock the chains that bind you. Let it remind you that true freedom comes from within, from seeing through the illusions and reclaiming your power. The path to freedom is not easy, but it is within your grasp if you are willing to face the truth."

The Fool felt a surge of determination and clarity as he took the key. He understood now that the journey was not just about avoiding temptation, but about confronting the illusions that held him back and breaking free from the chains of his own making.

The Departure

As the Fool prepared to leave, the Devil returned to his throne, his presence as dark and enigmatic as ever. "Go forth, traveler, and remember that the power to free yourself lies within you. Do not be swayed by the illusions of the world or the temptations that seek to bind you. Face your fears, confront your desires, and you will find the strength to break free and reclaim your true self."

The Fool bowed deeply, feeling a profound respect for the Devil's teachings. As he walked away from the cave, the silver key in his hand a reminder of the lessons he had learned, he felt a renewed sense of purpose and determination. He understood now that the journey was not just about avoiding the darkness, but about confronting it, seeing through the illusions, and finding the strength to break free.

With the Devil's teachings in mind, the Fool continued on his journey, ready to face the challenges of life with a clear mind and a strong heart. He knew that the road ahead would bring temptations and challenges that sought to bind him, but he also knew that with the power of truth and clarity, he could navigate these challenges and find true freedom.

And so, with the silver key as his guide, the Fool journeyed on, ready to face whatever the future held, knowing that with each step, he was moving closer to the fulfillment of his destiny, free from the chains of illusion and empowered by the truth of his own strength.

CHAPTER SEVENTEEN

THE TOWER - THE COLLAPSE OF ILLUSION

With the Devil's teachings on the chains of illusion and the power of freedom still fresh in his mind, the Fool continued his journey. The path ahead led him out of the shadowy cave and into a landscape that was stark and barren, marked by jagged rocks and a sky heavy with storm clouds. The air was thick with the scent of impending rain, and a sense of tension hung in the atmosphere, as if the world itself was holding its breath.

As the Fool walked, he noticed a towering structure in the distance—a tall, imposing tower that seemed to scrape the sky. The tower was built of stone, its walls high and seemingly impenetrable, but as the Fool drew closer, he saw that the foundation was cracked and unstable. The sky above the tower darkened, and lightning began to flash, illuminating the structure in brief, blinding bursts of light.

Suddenly, a bolt of lightning struck the tower with a deafening crack, and the Fool watched in shock as the top of the tower exploded in flames, the walls crumbling and collapsing in on themselves. The once-mighty tower was reduced to rubble in a matter of moments, its grandeur and strength revealed to be nothing more than an illusion.

This was the Tower, a symbol of sudden change, upheaval, and the collapse of false beliefs. It was a reminder that what is built on a foundation of illusion will inevitably fall, and that true transformation often comes through the destruction of the old to make way for the new.

The Meeting

As the dust settled, the Fool approached the remains of the tower, his heart pounding with the intensity of what he had just witnessed. Amid the rubble, he saw a figure standing tall and unscathed, a figure who radiated a calm acceptance of the destruction that had just occurred. This was the Tower Keeper, the guardian of transformation through upheaval, who understood the necessity of tearing down the old to build something stronger and more enduring.

"Welcome, traveler," the Tower Keeper said, their voice steady and resolute. "You have journeyed far and faced many trials, but now you stand before the inevitable collapse of illusion. What is it that you seek?"

The Fool, still shaken by the sight of the tower's destruction, replied, "I seek to understand the nature of sudden change, the destruction of what once seemed secure, and how to rebuild after everything has fallen apart. How can I find stability when the world around me is crumbling?"

The Lesson of Destruction and Rebirth

The Tower Keeper nodded, their gaze fixed on the ruins of the tower. "The tower you see before you was built on a foundation of illusion, of false beliefs and unstable truths. When the lightning struck, it revealed the weaknesses hidden beneath the surface, and the tower fell, as all things built on illusion must eventually do."

They gestured to the rubble, where small shoots of green were already beginning to push through the cracks. "But with destruction comes the opportunity for rebirth. The fall of the tower clears the way for new growth, for new structures built on a foundation of truth and integrity. The process may be painful, but it is necessary for true transformation."

The Fool listened closely, realizing that the Tower Keeper was teaching him about the importance of facing the truth, of allowing false beliefs and illusions to be destroyed, and of finding the strength to rebuild on a foundation of honesty and integrity.

The Advice

The Tower Keeper stepped closer, their presence strong and reassuring. "Remember, traveler, that destruction is not the end, but the beginning of something new. When the world around you crumbles, do not cling to the ruins of the past. Instead, look for the opportunities that arise from the ashes. Embrace the change, no matter how sudden or painful, and trust that what falls away is making room for something stronger, something more aligned with your true self."

They handed the Fool a small stone, smooth and solid, taken from the ruins of the tower. "Take this stone as a reminder that even in the midst of chaos, there is the seed of new beginnings. Let it remind you that the collapse of illusion is not a tragedy, but a necessary step in the journey of transformation. Rebuild with care, with truth, and with the wisdom gained from your experiences."

The Fool felt a deep sense of understanding and resolve as he took the stone. He understood now that the journey was not just about seeking stability, but about finding the strength to rebuild after everything has fallen apart, and about embracing the transformations that come through upheaval.

The Departure

As the Fool prepared to leave, the Tower Keeper returned to their place amid the ruins, their presence calm and unwavering. "Go forth, traveler, and remember that true strength lies not in avoiding change, but in embracing it. When the foundations of your life are shaken, do not fear the fall—welcome it as an opportunity to rebuild stronger, wiser, and more true to yourself. The path ahead may bring further challenges, but with each one, you will find yourself growing, evolving, and becoming more aligned with your highest purpose."

The Fool bowed deeply, feeling a profound respect for the Tower Keeper's teachings. As he walked away from the ruins, the stone in his hand a reminder of the lessons he had learned, he felt a renewed sense of purpose and determination. He understood now that the journey was not just about avoiding destruction, but about embracing the opportunities that arise from it, and about finding the strength to rebuild with integrity and truth.

With the Tower Keeper's teachings in mind, the Fool continued on his journey, ready to face the challenges of life with courage and resilience. He knew that the road ahead would bring both stability and upheaval, but he also knew that with the wisdom gained from each experience, he could navigate these challenges and emerge stronger on the other side.

And so, with the stone of transformation as his guide, the Fool journeyed on, ready to face whatever the future held, knowing that with each step, he was moving closer to the fulfillment of his destiny, free from the illusions of the past and empowered by the truth of his own strength.

CHAPTER EIGHTEEN

THE STAR - THE LIGHT OF HOPE

With the lessons of the Tower still resonating in his heart, the Fool continued his journey, walking away from the rubble and the remnants of what once was. The path ahead gradually led him away from the barren, storm-torn landscape into a place of quiet beauty and peace. The air was cool and refreshing, filled with the scent of wildflowers and the soft rustling of leaves. Above him, the sky had cleared, revealing a blanket of stars that twinkled like a thousand tiny beacons in the night.

As the Fool walked, he came upon a tranquil pool of water, its surface perfectly still, reflecting the starlight above. Kneeling by the water's edge was a figure of serene beauty, pouring water from two pitchers—one into the pool, and the other onto the earth. The figure was dressed in flowing robes that shimmered like the stars themselves, and around her head, a soft, radiant light seemed to glow.

This was the Star, the embodiment of hope, inspiration, and the healing light that guides us through the darkest times. Her presence was gentle and comforting, a reminder that even after the storm, there is always the promise of renewal and light.

The Meeting

As the Fool approached, the Star looked up, her eyes filled with warmth and compassion. "Welcome, traveler," she said, her voice like a melody carried on the breeze. "You have journeyed far and faced many trials, but now you stand at the place of hope and healing. What is it that you seek?"

The Fool, feeling a deep sense of peace in her presence, replied, "I seek to understand the power of hope, how to find light in the darkness, and how to heal from the wounds of the past. How can I continue my journey with a heart full of hope and a spirit renewed?"

The Lesson of Hope and Renewal

The Star smiled gently, her hands continuing their rhythmic motion, pouring the water that symbolized the flow of life and the continuous cycle of renewal. "Hope is the light that guides us through the darkest nights, the beacon that keeps us moving forward even when the path is unclear. It is the promise that no matter how difficult the journey, there is always the potential for renewal, for healing, and for new beginnings."

She gestured to the pool of water, where the stars reflected like tiny jewels. "Just as the stars shine their light from the heavens, hope shines within us, illuminating the path ahead. It is the force that keeps us connected to our dreams, our aspirations, and the vision of a better future. When we are wounded or lost, hope is the salve that heals, the energy that restores us to wholeness."

The Fool listened closely, realizing that the Star was teaching him about the importance of holding onto hope, of trusting in the process of healing, and of believing in the possibility of new beginnings.

The Advice

The Star stood, her presence graceful and soothing, and approached the Fool. She handed him one of the pitchers, its surface cool and smooth to the touch. "Remember, traveler, that hope is not a passive force, but an active choice. It is something we must cultivate, nurture, and pour into the world, just as I pour this water. When you face challenges or darkness, choose hope. Let it be the light that guides you, the strength that sustains you, and the inspiration that propels you forward."

She pointed to the stars above, their light steady and unwavering. "Take comfort in the knowledge that you are never truly alone. The stars above, the earth below, and the waters of life all flow together in a continuous cycle of renewal. Trust in this process, and know that even after the darkest night, the dawn will come, bringing with it the light of a new day."

The Fool felt a deep sense of hope and renewal as he took the pitcher. He understood now that the journey was not just about surviving the challenges of life, but about finding the light within, about holding onto hope and allowing it to guide him through the darkest times.

The Departure

As the Fool prepared to leave, the Star returned to her place by the water's edge, her hands continuing to pour the water of life. "Go forth, traveler, and remember that hope is the light that will guide you through all challenges. When you feel lost or weary, look to the stars, and let their light remind you of the infinite possibilities that lie ahead. Embrace the healing power of hope, and you will find that no matter how difficult the journey, there is always the promise of renewal and a brighter future."

The Fool bowed deeply, feeling a profound respect for the Star's teachings. As he walked away from the tranquil pool, the pitcher in his hand a reminder of the lessons he had learned, he felt a renewed sense of hope and optimism. He understood now that the journey was not just about overcoming obstacles, but about believing in the possibility of new beginnings, and about allowing hope to light the way.

With the Star's teachings in mind, the Fool continued on his journey, ready to face the challenges of life with a hopeful heart and a spirit renewed. He knew that the road ahead would bring both joy and sorrow, but he also knew that with the light of hope as his guide, he could navigate these challenges and emerge stronger, wiser, and more aligned with his true purpose.

And so, with the light of the stars shining above him and the pitcher of hope in his hand, the Fool journeyed on, ready to face whatever the future held, knowing that with each step, he was moving closer to the fulfillment of his destiny, guided by the eternal light of hope.

CHAPTER NINETEEN

THE MOON - THE REALM OF SHADOWS

With the Star's teachings of hope and renewal lighting his way, the Fool continued his journey, feeling uplifted and inspired. The path ahead led him into a landscape that gradually grew more mysterious and surreal. The clear night sky that had been filled with stars began to darken, and a thick mist began to roll in, obscuring the path and the surroundings.

As the mist enveloped him, the Fool felt the air grow colder and more humid. The light of the stars faded, leaving only a pale, eerie glow that seemed to emanate from all around him. The landscape took on a dreamlike quality, where shapes shifted and shadows danced at the edge of his vision. The only constant was the presence of a large, full moon, hanging low in the sky, its light casting long, distorted shadows over the landscape.

In the midst of this strange and unsettling place, the Fool noticed two figures—one was a dog, the other a wolf—both howling up at the moon. Between them stood a mysterious figure, draped in shadow, their face obscured by a hood. This was the Moon, the embodiment of illusion, mystery, and the unknown depths of the subconscious mind.

The Meeting

As the Fool approached, the Moon lifted its head, revealing a face that was both familiar and strange, a reflection of the Fool's own inner fears and desires. The Moon's voice was soft and echoing, as if coming from a great distance. "Welcome, traveler," the Moon said, its tone filled with a quiet intensity. "You have journeyed far and faced many trials, but now you stand at the edge of the unknown, where shadows and illusions reign. What is it that you seek?"

The Fool, feeling both intrigued and uneasy, replied, "I seek to understand the nature of illusion, the shadows that obscure the truth, and how to navigate the depths of the subconscious mind. How can I find my way when the path is hidden in darkness?"

The Lesson of Illusion and the Subconscious

The Moon smiled, a subtle, enigmatic expression that seemed to hold secrets untold. "The Moonlight reveals and obscures, casting shadows that can deceive the eye and the mind. This is the realm of the subconscious, where dreams and fears intertwine, where reality is blurred and the line between truth and illusion is thin."

The Moon gestured to the mist that surrounded them, its tendrils curling and shifting like living things. "In this place, you must rely not on what you see, but on what you feel. The path ahead may be hidden, but it is there, waiting to be discovered. To navigate the realm of shadows, you must trust your intuition, listen to the whispers of your inner voice, and confront the fears that dwell within your own soul."

The Fool listened closely, realizing that the Moon was teaching him about the importance of understanding the subconscious mind, of exploring the hidden depths within himself, and of learning to trust his instincts in the face of uncertainty.

The Advice

The Moon stepped closer, the shadows shifting and swirling around it, giving the impression that the figure was both present and distant. "Remember, traveler, that the unknown can be both terrifying and enlightening. It is in the shadows that we often find the truths we seek, the insights that have been hidden from our conscious mind. Do not fear the darkness, for it is a part of you, just as much as the light."

The Moon handed the Fool a small, silver mirror, its surface smooth and reflective. "Take this mirror as a tool for reflection, both literal and metaphorical. Let it remind you to look beyond the surface, to see the truth that lies beneath the illusions. Use it to explore your own subconscious, to confront your fears, and to find clarity in the midst of uncertainty."

The Fool felt a deep sense of introspection and understanding as he took the mirror. He understood now that the journey was not just about navigating the external world, but about exploring the depths of his own mind, confronting the illusions that clouded his vision, and finding the truth within.

The Departure

As the Fool prepared to leave, the Moon returned to its place among the shadows, its presence ethereal and elusive. "Go forth, traveler, and remember that the path to truth is often hidden in the shadows. Embrace the mystery, explore the unknown, and trust in your intuition to guide you through the darkness. The journey ahead may be filled with illusions, but with clarity of mind and heart, you will find your way."

The Fool bowed deeply, feeling a profound respect for the Moon's teachings. As he walked away from the misty landscape, the silver mirror in his hand a reminder of the lessons he had learned, he felt a renewed sense of purpose and clarity. He understood now that the journey was not just about avoiding the unknown, but about embracing it, about delving into the depths of his own psyche, and about finding the truth that lay hidden in the shadows.

With the Moon's teachings in mind, the Fool continued on his journey, ready to face the challenges of life with a clear mind and a strong heart. He knew that the road ahead would bring both clarity and confusion, light and darkness, but he also knew that with the wisdom gained from each experience, he could navigate these challenges and emerge stronger, wiser, and more aligned with his true self.

And so, with the silver mirror as his guide, the Fool journeyed on, ready to explore the depths of the unknown, to confront the illusions that lay in wait, and to find the truth that would lead him ever closer to the fulfillment of his destiny.

CHAPTER TWENTY

THE SUN - THE DAWN OF CLARITY

Emerging from the shadows of the Moon's realm, the Fool continued his journey, now carrying with him a deep understanding of the illusions and mysteries that had once clouded his path. The mist began to lift, and the darkness gave way to the first light of dawn. The air grew warmer, and the landscape gradually transformed into one of vibrant color and life. Flowers bloomed, birds sang, and the world seemed to awaken around him.

As the sun rose higher in the sky, its golden rays illuminated the path ahead, filling the Fool with a sense of warmth and optimism. In the distance, he saw a figure standing in a field of sunflowers, bathed in the radiant light of the morning sun. The figure was a child, full of joy and innocence, riding a white horse. Around the child's head was a crown of flowers, and in their hand, they held a bright red banner that fluttered in the gentle breeze.

This was the Sun, the embodiment of clarity, enlightenment, and the pure joy of life. The Sun's presence was bright and welcoming, a beacon of truth and positivity after the long journey through the darkness.

The Meeting

As the Fool approached, the Sun turned to greet him, the child's face beaming with happiness and warmth. "Welcome, traveler," the Sun said, their voice filled with the lightness of a clear day. "You have journeyed far and faced many trials, but now you stand in the light of truth and clarity. What is it that you seek?"

The Fool, feeling a surge of joy and relief in the Sun's presence, replied, "I seek to understand the nature of truth, the light that dispels the darkness, and how to live with clarity and joy. How can I embrace the fullness of life and let the light guide my way?"

The Lesson of Clarity and Joy

The Sun laughed gently, the sound like the tinkling of bells carried on the wind. "The light of the Sun reveals all things, casting away the shadows and bringing everything into the open. It is the light of truth, of clarity, that allows us to see the world as it truly is, free from the distortions of fear and doubt."

The Sun gestured to the field of sunflowers, all facing the bright orb in the sky. "Just as the flowers turn to follow the Sun, so too must you turn towards the light of truth. Embrace the clarity it brings, the understanding that comes from seeing things as they are. In this light, there is no room for illusion, only the pure joy of living in harmony with the world around you."

The Fool listened closely, realizing that the Sun was teaching him about the importance of living with honesty, openness, and a joyful heart. The journey through darkness had led him to this moment of enlightenment, where he could see clearly and embrace the beauty of life.

The Advice

The Sun stepped closer, the warmth of their presence enveloping the Fool like a comforting embrace. "Remember, traveler, that clarity and joy are your birthrights. They are the gifts of living in alignment with your true self, of embracing the light and letting it guide your way. When you face challenges or doubts, turn to the light of truth, and let it illuminate the path ahead."

The Sun handed the Fool the bright red banner, its fabric vibrant and alive with color. "Take this banner as a symbol of your victory over darkness, your triumph in the journey towards truth and clarity. Let it remind you to celebrate life, to live with an open heart, and to spread the light wherever you go. The world is a beautiful place, full of wonder and joy, and it is yours to explore and embrace."

The Fool felt a deep sense of happiness and fulfillment as he took the banner. He understood now that the journey was not just about seeking the light, but about living in it, about embracing the joy and clarity that come from living in harmony with the truth.

The Departure

As the Fool prepared to leave, the Sun returned to their place in the field of flowers, their presence radiant and joyful. "Go forth, traveler, and remember that the light of the Sun is always with you. Let it guide you, inspire you, and fill your life with warmth and clarity. The journey ahead is bright, full of possibilities and new adventures, and with the light of the Sun, you will find that there is nothing you cannot achieve."

The Fool bowed deeply, feeling a profound respect for the Sun's teachings. As he walked away from the field of sunflowers, the red banner in his hand a reminder of the lessons he had learned, he felt a renewed sense of purpose and optimism. He understood now that the journey was not just about overcoming darkness, but about living fully in the light, about embracing the truth and joy that life had to offer.

With the Sun's teachings in mind, the Fool continued on his journey, ready to face the challenges of life with a clear mind and a joyful heart. He knew that the road ahead would bring both triumph and trials, but he also knew that with the light of clarity and the warmth of joy, he could navigate these challenges and emerge stronger, wiser, and more aligned with his true self.

And so, with the banner of victory as his guide, the Fool journeyed on, ready to embrace the fullness of life, to spread the light wherever he went, and to continue his journey towards the fulfillment of his destiny, guided by the eternal light of the Sun.

CHAPTER TWENTY-ONE

JUDGMENT - THE CALL TO AWAKENING

With the light of the Sun filling his heart with joy and clarity, the Fool continued his journey, feeling more aligned with his true self than ever before. The path ahead seemed brighter, and the world around him felt alive with possibility. But as he walked, the landscape began to shift once again. The vibrant colors of the sunlit fields gradually gave way to a more somber, ethereal realm, where the air was still and the sky was tinged with the soft glow of twilight.

In this quiet, liminal space, the Fool heard a sound—a distant, echoing call that seemed to resonate deep within his soul. The sound grew louder as he continued on, and soon he saw the source of the call: a figure standing atop a hill, blowing a long, golden trumpet. The figure was angelic, their wings spread wide, and their presence radiated a sense of authority and purpose.

Below the angel, emerging from the ground, were figures that seemed to rise from their slumber, answering the call of the trumpet. These figures were bathed in a soft, golden light, their faces turned upward in anticipation and reverence. This was the scene of Judgment, a powerful moment of awakening, of reckoning, and of the call to a higher purpose.

The Meeting

As the Fool approached, the angel lowered the trumpet and looked down upon him with eyes that seemed to see into the very depths of his being. "Welcome, traveler," the angel said, their voice resonant and clear, like a bell ringing across the land. "You have journeyed far and faced many trials, but now you stand at the threshold of awakening, where the call of your higher self beckons you forward. What is it that you seek?"

The Fool, feeling a deep sense of reverence in the angel's presence, replied, "I seek to understand the nature of judgment, the call to awaken to my true purpose, and how to answer that call with courage and clarity. How can I rise to meet the challenges of my higher self?"

The Lesson of Awakening and Purpose

The angel nodded, their expression both compassionate and firm. "Judgment is the call to awaken to your true self, to rise above the illusions and limitations of the past and embrace your higher purpose. It is a moment of reckoning, where you are called to account for your actions, your choices, and the life you have lived. But it is also a moment of renewal, of rebirth, where you are given the opportunity to step into the fullness of who you are meant to be."

They gestured to the figures rising from the earth, their faces filled with a sense of awe and recognition. "These souls are answering the call of their higher selves, awakening to the truth of their existence and the purpose they are meant to fulfill. In your journey, you too are called to awaken, to leave behind the shadows of the past and step into the light of your true potential."

The Fool listened intently, realizing that the angel was teaching him about the importance of self-reflection, of taking responsibility for his actions, and of embracing the call to a higher purpose.

The Advice

The angel stepped closer, their presence both powerful and gentle. "Remember, traveler, that the call to awakening is not one to be feared, but one to be embraced with courage and humility. It is an invitation to rise above the limitations of the past, to release the burdens that have held you back, and to step into the light of your true self."

The angel handed the Fool a small, golden trumpet, its surface gleaming in the twilight. "Take this trumpet as a symbol of the call to awakening that echoes within you. Let it remind you to listen to the voice of your higher self, to answer the call with courage and clarity, and to step into the purpose for which you were born. The journey ahead is one of renewal, of transformation, and of stepping into the fullness of who you are meant to be."

The Fool felt a deep sense of responsibility and purpose as he took the trumpet. He understood now that the journey was not just about seeking knowledge or achieving goals, but about answering the call to his higher self, about embracing his true purpose and living in alignment with the divine plan.

The Departure

As the Fool prepared to leave, the angel returned to their place atop the hill, their presence glowing with a soft, golden light. "Go forth, traveler, and remember that the call to awakening is a gift, a moment of grace where you are given the opportunity to step into the light of your true self. Answer the call with courage, with clarity, and with a heart open to the possibilities of your higher purpose. The path ahead may be challenging, but with each step, you will find yourself rising higher, closer to the fulfillment of your destiny."

The Fool bowed deeply, feeling a profound respect for the angel's teachings. As he walked away from the hill, the golden trumpet in his hand a reminder of the lessons he had learned, he felt a renewed sense of purpose and determination. He understood now that the journey was not just about overcoming obstacles, but about answering the call to his higher self, about rising to meet the challenges of his purpose with courage and clarity.

With the angel's teachings in mind, the Fool continued on his journey, ready to face the challenges of life with a clear mind and a strong heart. He knew that the road ahead would bring both trials and triumphs, but he also knew that with the call to awakening guiding his way, he could navigate these challenges and emerge stronger, wiser, and more aligned with his true self.

And so, with the trumpet of awakening as his guide, the Fool journeyed on, ready to embrace his higher purpose, to answer the call of his soul, and to continue his journey towards the fulfillment of his destiny, guided by the light of his true self and the divine purpose that called him forward.

CHAPTER TWENTY-TWO

THE WORLD - THE COMPLETION OF THE JOURNEY

With the golden trumpet of awakening in hand, the Fool continued his journey, feeling a profound sense of purpose and determination. The landscape around him began to change, growing more vibrant and alive with each step. The path ahead became clearer, the air warmer and filled with the scent of blooming flowers and the sounds of life in full celebration.

As he walked, the Fool noticed a circle of light in the distance, shimmering like a portal. As he drew closer, the circle expanded, revealing a figure at its center. This figure was a beautiful androgynous being, draped in flowing robes that seemed to be woven from the very fabric of the universe. They held a wand in each hand, symbolizing the balance and unity of all things.

Around the figure, the circle was bordered by the four elements, represented by a lion, an eagle, a bull, and an angel. These symbols signified the completion of the Fool's journey through the material and spiritual realms, the integration of all that he had learned and experienced.

This was the World, the final stage of the Fool's journey, representing completion, fulfillment, and the harmony of all aspects of existence.

The Meeting

As the Fool stepped into the circle of light, the World greeted him with a radiant smile, their eyes filled with the wisdom of the ages. "Welcome, traveler," the World said, their voice resonant and soothing, as if echoing from the very core of creation. "You have journeyed far, faced many trials, and now you stand at the threshold of completion. What is it that you seek?"

The Fool, feeling a deep sense of accomplishment and peace, replied, "I seek to understand the nature of fulfillment, the completion of my journey, and how to live in harmony with the world and myself. How can I embrace the wholeness of existence and continue to grow beyond this moment?"

The Lesson of Fulfillment and Unity

The World nodded, their expression serene and understanding. "The World is the culmination of all your experiences, the integration of all that you have learned and become. It is the moment of fulfillment, where you realize that you are a part of something greater, a thread in the vast tapestry of existence. This is the place where all things come together in perfect harmony."

They gestured to the four symbols that surrounded them, representing the elements of earth, air, fire, and water. "These elements, these forces of nature, are all within you, just as they are within the world. You have journeyed through them, learned their lessons, and now you stand in the center, in balance with all that is. The journey you have taken has brought you here, to this place of unity and wholeness."

The Fool listened closely, realizing that the World was teaching him about the importance of embracing the entirety of his journey, of understanding that every step, every challenge, every moment of joy and sorrow had led him to this place of fulfillment.

The Advice

The World stepped closer, their presence warm and embracing, like the gentle arms of the universe itself. "Remember, traveler, that the journey does not end here. Completion is not a final destination, but a new beginning. The World is a circle, ever-turning, ever-evolving, and so too are you. Embrace the wholeness of your being, the integration of all that you have learned, and know that you are now ready to step into the world with confidence and grace."

They handed the Fool one of the wands, its surface glowing with a soft, inner light. "Take this wand as a symbol of your mastery, your ability to create and shape your own destiny. Let it remind you that you are a part of the world, connected to all things, and that your journey continues in new and wondrous ways. The world is yours to explore, to contribute to, and to cherish."

The Fool felt a deep sense of fulfillment and unity as he took the wand. He understood now that the journey was not just about reaching an end, but about realizing the interconnectedness of all things, about living in harmony with the world and continuing to grow and evolve.

The Departure

As the Fool prepared to leave, the World returned to their place within the circle, their presence radiant and all-encompassing. "Go forth, traveler, and remember that you are a part of the world, a vital piece of the great tapestry of existence. Embrace the wholeness of who you are, the unity of all that you have become, and step into the world with a heart full of love, a mind full of wisdom, and a spirit ready for new adventures. The journey ahead is infinite, and with each step, you will find new paths, new opportunities, and new ways to grow."

The Fool bowed deeply, feeling a profound respect for the World's teachings. As he walked away from the circle of light, the wand in his hand a reminder of the lessons he had learned, he felt a renewed sense of purpose and clarity. He understood now that the journey was not just about completing a cycle, but about embracing the endless possibilities that lay ahead, about continuing to grow and evolve in harmony with the world.

With the World's teachings in mind, the Fool continued on his journey, ready to face the challenges and opportunities of life with a clear mind, a loving heart, and a spirit full of wonder. He knew that the road ahead would bring both familiar and new experiences, but he also knew that with the wisdom gained from his journey, he could navigate these experiences with grace and confidence.

And so, with the wand of mastery as his guide, the Fool journeyed on, ready to embrace the infinite possibilities of the world, to contribute to the harmony of all things, and to continue his journey towards the fulfillment of his destiny, now as a part of the great, ever-turning circle of life.

Epilogue: The Fool's New Beginning

Having completed the journey through the tarot, the Fool stood at the edge of a new path, his heart filled with wisdom, his spirit buoyed by the lessons he had learned. He had encountered the Magician's mastery, the High Priestess's intuition, the Empress's nurturing love, the Emperor's authority, and all the others who had guided him along the way. Now, standing at the threshold of his next adventure, the Fool realized that the journey was far from over; it was only just beginning.

The World had taught him that completion is not an end but a gateway to new possibilities, and so the Fool stood ready to embark on this new phase with an open heart and a clear mind. He no longer carried the naivety of his earlier days, but a deeper understanding of the cycles of life, the power of choice, and the importance of balance, transformation, and awakening.

As he looked ahead, the path before him stretched out into the distance, winding through landscapes both familiar and new. The sun was shining brightly, casting a warm glow over the world, and in the sky above, a single bird soared high, a symbol of freedom and the limitless potential that lay before him.

The Fool's Realization

In this moment of quiet reflection, the Fool realized that he was no longer the same person who had set out on this journey. He had been transformed by his experiences, each encounter adding to the tapestry of his soul. He understood now that the Fool's journey was not a linear path, but a spiral, ever-evolving and deepening with each turn. The end of one cycle simply marked the beginning of another, each new beginning richer and more profound than the last.

He also recognized that the Fool was not just a card in the tarot or a role to be played; the Fool was an archetype within us all, the part of us that is always learning, always growing, and always seeking the next adventure. The Fool was the eternal seeker, the one who dares to step into the unknown with faith and curiosity, knowing that each step is a step toward greater understanding and self-discovery.

The New Beginning

With this realization, the Fool took a deep breath and stepped forward onto the new path. He carried with him the tools and symbols he had gathered along the way—the Magician's wand, the High Priestess's scroll, the Empress's fruit, the Emperor's stone, the Hierophant's key, the Lovers' choice, the Chariot's reins, Strength's garland, the Hermit's lantern, the Wheel of Fortune's token, Justice's scales, the Hanged Man's insight, Death's rose, Temperance's cup, the Devil's key, the Tower's stone, the Star's pitcher, the Moon's mirror, the Sun's banner, and the World's wand. Each one was a reminder of the lessons he had learned, the challenges he had faced, and the wisdom he had gained.

But more than these physical symbols, the Fool carried within him the deeper understanding that life is a journey of continuous growth and transformation. He knew that as he continued to walk this path, he would encounter new challenges, new teachers, and new opportunities for growth. And he welcomed these with an open heart, knowing that each step would bring him closer to the fulfillment of his destiny.

The Eternal Journey

As the Fool walked on, the landscape around him began to change once more, but this time, he did not look back with longing or regret. He had learned to embrace change, to welcome the unknown, and to trust in the process of life. He knew that wherever the path led, he would face it with courage, wisdom, and a spirit of adventure.

And so, the Fool continued on his journey, knowing that the lessons he had learned would serve as his guide, and that the world was full of endless possibilities just waiting to be discovered. With each step, he felt a sense of joy and anticipation, eager to see what new adventures awaited him.

For the Fool's journey is never truly over. It is an eternal quest, a cycle of learning, growth, and renewal that continues throughout the course of life. And with each new beginning, the Fool sets out once more, ready to face whatever challenges and opportunities come his way, knowing that the journey itself is the greatest adventure of all.